PERCY AND HAROLD

by

The Rev. W. Awdry

with illustrations by
C. Reginald Dalby and John T. Kenney

Grolier

Percy and Harold

PERCY worked hard at the Harbour. Toby helped, but sometimes the loads of stone were too heavy, and Percy had to fetch them for himself. Then he would push the trucks along the quay to where the workmen needed the stone for their building.

An airfield was close by, and Percy heard the aeroplanes zooming overhead all day. The noisiest of all was a helicopter, which hovered, buzzing like an angry bee.

"Stupid thing!" said Percy, "why can't it go and buzz somewhere else?"

One day Percy stopped near the airfield. The helicopter was standing quite close.

"Hullo!" said Percy, "who are you?"

"I'm Harold, who are you?"

"I'm Percy. What whirly great arms you've got."

"They're nice arms," said Harold, offended. "I can hover like a bird. Don't you wish *you* could hover?"

"Certainly not; I like my rails, thank you."

"I think railways are slow," said Harold in a bored voice. "They're not much use, and quite out of date." He whirled his arms and buzzed away.

Percy found Toby at the Top Station arranging trucks.

"I say, Toby," he burst out, "that Harold, that stuck-up whirlibird thing, says I'm slow and out of date. Just let him wait, I'll show him!"

He collected his trucks and started off, still fuming.

Soon above the clatter of the trucks they heard a familiar buzzing.

"Percy," whispered his Driver, "there's Harold. He's not far ahead. Let's race him."

"Yes, let's," said Percy excitedly, and quickly gathering speed, he shot off down the line.

The Guard's wife had given him a flask of tea for "elevenses". He had just poured out a cup when the Van lurched and he spilt it down his uniform. He wiped up the mess with his handkerchief, and staggered to the front platform.

Percy was pounding along, the trucks screamed and swayed, while the Van rolled and pitched like a ship at sea.

"Well, I'll be ding-dong-danged!" said the Guard.

Then he saw Harold buzzing alongside, and understood.

"Go it, Percy!" he yelled. "You're gaining."

Percy had never been allowed to run fast before; he was having the time of his life!

"Hurry! Hurry! Hurry!" he panted to the trucks.

"We-don't-want-to; we-don't-want-to," they grumbled; but it was no use, Percy was bucketing along with flying wheels, and Harold was high and alongside.

The Fireman shovelled for dear life, while the Driver was so excited he could hardly keep still.

"Well done, Percy," he shouted, "we're gaining! We're going ahead! Oh good boy, good boy!"

Far ahead, a "distant signal" warned them that the Wharf was near. Shut off steam, whistle, "Peep, peep, peep, brakes, Guard, please." Using Percy's brakes too, the Driver carefully checked the train's headlong speed. They rolled under the main line, and halted smoothly on the Wharf.

"Oh dear!" groaned Percy, "I'm sure we've lost."

The Fireman scrambled to the cab roof. "We've won! we've won!" he shouted and nearly fell off in his excitement.

"Harold's still hovering. He's looking for a place to land!"

"Listen boys!" the Fireman called. "Here's a song for Percy."

Said Harold helicopter to our Percy, "You are slow!

Your Railway is out of date and not much use, you know."

But Percy, with his stone-trucks, did the trip in record time;

And we beat that helicopter on Our Old Branch Line.

The Driver and Guard soon caught the tune, and so did the workmen on the quay.
Percy loved it. "Oh thank you!" he said. He liked the last line best of all.

Percy takes the Plunge

SOMETIMES Percy takes stone trucks to the other end of the line. There, he meets engines from the Other Railway.

One day, Henry wanted to rest in the shed; but Percy was talking to some tank-engines.

" . . . It was raining hard. Water swirled under my boiler. I couldn't see where I was going; but I struggled on."

"Ooooh Percy, you *are* brave."

"Well," said Percy modestly, "it wasn't anything really. Water's nothing to an engine with determination."

"Tell us more, Percy," said the engines.

"What are you engines doing here?" hissed Henry. "This shed is for the Fat Controller's Engines. Go away.

"Silly things," Henry snorted.

"They're not silly." Percy had been enjoying himself. He was cross because Henry had sent them away.

"They are silly, and so are you. 'Water's nothing to an engine with determination.' Pah!"

"Anyway," said cheeky Percy, "I'm not afraid of water. I like it." He ran away singing,

"Once an engine attached to a train
Was afraid of a few drops of rain . . . ."

Percy arrived home feeling pleased with himself. "Silly old Henry," he chuckled.

Thomas was looking at a board on the Quay. It said "DANGER".

"We mustn't go past it," he said. "That's Orders."

"Why?"

" 'DANGER' means falling down something," said Thomas. "I went past 'DANGER' once, and fell down a mine."

Percy looked beyond the board. "I can't see a mine," he said. He didn't know that the foundations of the Quay had sunk, and that the rails now sloped downward to the sea.

"Stupid board!" said Percy. For days and days he tried to sidle past it; but his Driver stopped him every time.

"No you don't," he would say.

Then Percy made a plan.

One day at the Top station he whispered to the trucks, "Will you give me a bump when we get to the Quay?"

The trucks were surprised. They had never been asked to bump an engine before. They giggled and chattered about it the whole way down.

"Whoah Percy! Whoah!" said his Driver, and Percy checked obediently at the Distant signal.

"Driver doesn't know my plan," he chuckled.

"On! On! On!" laughed the trucks. Percy thought they were helping. "I'll pretend to stop at the station; but the trucks will push me past the board. Then I'll make them stop. I can do that whenever I like."

If Percy hadn't been so conceited, he would never have been so silly. Every wise engine knows that you cannot trust trucks.

They reached the station, and Percy's brakes groaned. That was the signal for the trucks.

"Go on! Go on!" they yelled, and surged forward together.

They gave Percy a fearful bump, and knocked his Driver and Fireman off the footplate.

"Ow!" said Percy, sliding past the board.

The day was misty. The rails were slippery. His wheels wouldn't grip.

Percy was frantic. "That's enough!" he hissed.

But it was too late. Once on the slope, he tobogganed helplessly down, crashed through the buffers, and slithered into the sea.

"You are a very disobedient engine."

Percy knew that voice. He groaned.

The Foreman borrowed a small boat and rowed the Fat Controller round.

"Please, Sir, get me out Sir, I'm truly sorry Sir."

"No, Percy, we cannot do that till high tide. I hope it will teach you to obey Orders."

"Yes, Sir," Percy shivered miserably. He was cold. Fish were playing hide and seek through his wheels. The tide rose higher and higher.

He was feeling his position more and more deeply every minute.

It was nearly dark when they brought floating cranes, cleared away the trucks, and lifted Percy out. He was too cold and stiff to move by himself, so he was sent to the Works next day on Henry's goods train.

"Well! Well! Well!" chuckled Henry, "Did you like the water?"

"No."

"I *am* surprised. You need more determination, Percy. 'Water's nothing to an engine with determination' you know. Perhaps you will like it better next time."

But Percy is quite determined that there won't be a "next time".

This book club edition published by Grolier 1995

Published by arrangement with Reed Children's Books
The story *Percy and Harold* first published in Great Britain 1956 as part of *The Railway Series* No. 11
Copyright © William Heinemann Ltd. 1956
The story *Percy Takes the Plunge* first published in Great Britain 1957 as part of *The Railway Series* No. 12
Copyright © William Heinemann Ltd. 1957
This edition copyright © William Heinemann Ltd. 1995